Room of Doom

Adapted by M.C. King

Based on the television series, "The Suite Life of Zack & Cody", created by Danny Kallis & Jim Geoghan

Based on the episode written by Pamela Eels O'Connell

New York

Printed in the United States of America

First Edition
3 5 7 9 10 8 6 4 2

Library of Congress Catalog Card Number on file.

ISBN 0-7868-4937-1
For more Disney Press fun, visit www.disneybooks.com
Visit DisneyChannel.com

Chapter 1

The room was a mess. On every single surface, on every piece of furniture, lay a pile of something. There was a pile of dirty laundry, a pile of schoolbooks and papers, even an enormous pile of pillows—although Zack and Cody Martin liked to think of that particular pile as a fort. The fluffy down pillows at the Tipton Hotel made the best pillow forts.

The Tipton was just about the fanciest hotel in Boston, and Zack and Cody were proud to call it home. Who wouldn't be? The Tipton had a rooftop pool with a Jacuzzi, a well-stocked candy counter in the lobby, and a game room in the basement. There was twenty-four-hour room service, which meant ice cream anytime—not to mention cheeseburgers and turkey clubs. How had Zack and Cody gotten so lucky? Well, their mother, Carey, was a professional singer who'd been hired to perform regularly in the hotel ballroom. A beautiful rent-free suite on the twenty-third floor was one of the perks of the job.

Zack and Cody were twins. They were almost identical, but not quite. They each had blond hair and blue eyes, and they were around the same height. Really, it was their personalities that set them apart. Zack was the more fun-loving of the brothers; Cody, the more serious. Zack liked to think it was because he was so much older—in fact, he was a whole ten minutes older!—that he was more willing to take a dare or play a prank. Zack liked to think he was the fearless brother.

Still, he had to admit he flinched when from inside the pillow fort he heard the suite door open, and the menacing sound of his mother's footsteps. Carey had a lovely voice when it came to singing, but when it came to screaming, she was downright frightful. And that big pile of pillows did nothing to muffle her high-pitched yell. "Guys, get out here!"

Zack didn't move. Instead, he remained motionless inside the pillow fort, while Cody—who'd been in the bedroom—emerged to confront Carey alone. "Yeah,

Mom?" Zack heard Cody say in his most innocent voice.

Zack couldn't see, but he imagined Carey had her hands on her hips. And he didn't have to see her to hear the determination in her voice. "When I left, there was a room under this mess. I'd like it back. So start cleaning." He listened with relief as his mother left the room and Cody let out a bitter sigh.

"Great, next thing you know she's gonna make me take a bath," Zack heard his brother grumble. Then, an idea struck Zack, and he couldn't resist acting on it. He peered between the pillows to see Cody sorting through a pile of clothes. Then, with expert precision and speed, he reached his hand out to grab his unsuspecting brother's wrist in a death grip.

Cody shrieked, then scrambled backward

in terror, finally falling into a pile of dirty laundry.

"Gotcha!" Zack shouted triumphantly, busting out from the pillow fort.

Cody's eyes glazed over in fury, and he grabbed Zack and wrestled him to the ground. "Got *you*!" he yelled back.

It was just then that Carey reentered. "Cody, why are you cleaning the carpet with your brother's face? Although if it gets the stain out . . ."

Zack was thinking his plan worked brilliantly: not only had he scared the wits out of Cody, he'd gotten him in trouble, too! Only Cody turned it around. "Mommy," the younger twin whimpered, "Zack scared me again."

"Zack!" Carey's voice was scolding. "You know Cody is sensitive. Why do you try to scare him?"

"It's my job," Zack said, trying not to sound too smug about it.

"Well, you're fired," Carey told him. Exasperated, she left the two brothers to clean up their mess.

Chapter 2

Spooking Cody had gotten Zack's adrenaline pounding, and while cleaning up, he plotted his next attack. This time, he was going to pull a real prank. His victim? Esteban, the Tipton's trusted bellhop.

Zack entered the lobby to find Cody, Maddie, and London converged at the candy counter. Maddie Fitzpatrick had an after-school job working at the candy counter.

London Tipton (as in the Tipton Hotel) had never worked a day in her life. Like the twins, London lived in the hotel—only her suite was decked out to meet her every decorating whim. Plus, it was a lot roomier.

"Hey, guys! Watch this," Zack told the group. He pointed the remote control in the direction of Esteban, who was assisting an elegant couple checking in to the hotel.

Just as Esteban went to pick up the couple's luggage, a noise that seemed to come from his backside went: *Pffffffftttttttttttt!!!*"

A flustered Esteban dropped the luggage. "No . . . oh, no! That was not me!" he told the horrified-looking couple.

He bent over once more to pick up the luggage.

"*Pffffffftttttttttttt!!! Pffffffftttttttttttt!!!*"

The noises coming from Esteban were attracting lots of aghast looks. Almost the entire lobby had turned toward him in horror. The ever-efficient hotel manager, Mr. Moseby, rushed over to quiet the situation. "Esteban," he whispered, "you may excuse yourself."

"*Pffffffttttttttttt!!! Pffffffttttttttttt!!!*"

"Quickly, please," Mr. Moseby pleaded. "We'll discuss your dietary habits later."

"Mr. Moseby," Esteban sputtered, "the gassy noises is not me."

Mr. Moseby cast an apologetic look toward the elegant couple, then lifted his nose derisively toward Esteban. "Leave," he commanded.

As Esteban departed, the noises continued. "*Pfffttt!!! Pfffttt!!!*" He passed the group at the candy counter who could no longer hold back their laughter.

Esteban may have been humiliated, but he wasn't dumb. It didn't take him long to put two and two together. He kept his eyes on the laughing kids and reached into his jacket pocket to discover . . . a fart machine. He knew immediately who the culprit was. "Zack, I'm getting a little tired of your impractical jokes," he said, wagging his finger angrily.

Zack apologized, but his meek "Sorry" didn't sound so convincing. And as Esteban stalked off, Zack just couldn't help hitting the remote one last time.

"*Pffffffttttttttt!!!*"

"Man, that was awesome!" hooted Zack, sounding awfully proud of himself. "Almost as funny as this morning when Cody got so scared."

"I wasn't scared," Cody protested, not too convincingly.

"You were white as a sheet!" argued Zack.

The twins' squabbling was interrupted by London's dramatic gasp. "Don't tell me," she groaned, her heavily made-up eyes widening, "you saw the ghost in Suite 613."

Cody appeared paralyzed as he processed this information. A ghost? In suite 613? In the hotel? This hotel? Zack, of course, took this new information in stride. "There's a ghost in the hotel? Cool!" He gave his brother a taunting look. "Let's go see it."

"Uh, maybe later," Cody hedged.

"What's the matter? Afraid?"

Cody muttered something about just having had lunch, and how he had to wait an hour before "diving into the super-natural."

Sensible Maddie jumped in. "There's no

such thing as ghosts," she informed the group.

"Wrong as usual," countered London in a singsong voice. "I've seen this ghost. It was so scary, I dropped my new purse and left it there."

The rest of them stared at her in shock. "With money in it?" asked Maddie. As hard as she worked, Maddie was always strapped for cash.

"Just the regular thousand-dollar bill every kid gets for her allowance," London replied matter-of-factly.

That was all the information they needed. Cody, Zack, and Maddie bounded toward the elevator without looking back. A crisp thousand-dollar bill was good incentive to visit the ghost in Suite 613—even for fearful Cody and levelheaded Maddie.

"Hey, just because I don't need it doesn't

mean it's not mine!" London called out. They ignored her. And so, she sprinted ahead to catch up.

She was pretty fast for a girl wearing four-inch-high heels.

Chapter 3

They huffed and puffed their way down the sixth-floor hallway, so delirious they smacked right into a housekeeping cart, sending towels and miniature shampoo bottles flying. "Hey, watch it!" the housekeeper, Muriel, scolded. "I got three clock radios and a DVD player hidden in here."

"Where's Suite 613?" Zack asked breathlessly.

Muriel quickly went from annoyed to

concerned. "Over there," she said, lowering her voice and pointing in the direction of the suite. "But if you value your life, don't go in there. . . ."

Muriel's warning had the opposite effect on Zack and Cody.

"Let's go!" boomed Zack.

"Let's not!" cowered Cody.

Zack pushed Cody toward the room. Cody pushed Zack away from it, and right back into Muriel's cart. Muriel looked fierce as she tried to steady the wobbling cart. Now she'd do *anything* to rid herself of these two. "On second thought," she grumbled, reaching into her pocket, "here's the key."

Before Muriel could get away, London asked her to tell the rest of the group about the ghost. It was a good story, so Muriel agreed.

"Her name was Irene and she was

beautiful and rich," the housekeeper began.

"Oooh, like me!" interrupted London. "Except with less money. And probably not as pretty." She looked contemplative for a second, then added, "And dead."

Muriel glared at London, rolled her eyes, then continued. "As *I* was saying, in 1942 Irene and her husband checked in for their honeymoon night and the next day—"

London just couldn't help herself. She rudely interrupted again. "He went off to war! She waited three years, and he never came back."

"So he died in battle?" asked Zack.

"Oh, no, he—" corrected London.

This time Muriel interrupted London—by stuffing a feather duster in her lip-glossed mouth. "He met some Italian babe and opened a pizza place in Naples," Muriel told them.

London managed to extract the feather duster from her mouth. "Irene was so angry, she threw the silver hairbrush he'd given her at the mirror!" She sprayed feathers as she talked.

"And the mirror shattered and a shard flew out and that was the end of that." Muriel made a dramatic motion with her hand across her throat to let them know that poor Irene had met a gruesome death: a piece of the mirror had sliced her throat.

Moments later, Muriel headed down the hallway with her cart, and the group found its way to Suite 613.

They stood in front of the door. "I can't get it open," Maddie groaned while struggling with the key Muriel had given them.

"What a shame. Let's go," quipped Cody, pleased for the opportunity to get away. But just as the rest of the group began to follow him, they heard a creak. They turned back to see that the door to Suite 613 had mysteriously opened.

"It's the ghost," gasped London, ducking behind Cody for protection. Of course, an equally rattled Cody would have sooner ducked behind her.

"It is not," said Maddie, who seemed to have an answer for everything today. "We obviously loosened the lock, and the wind opened it up."

At that, the door slammed open, and the ghost-hunters entered the room.

Chapter 4

Cobwebs stretched from one end of the suite to the other: from the threadbare couch to the fogged-up window; across the old yellowed keys on the grand piano; from the golden candelabra to the ancient-looking statues. White dust cloths hung across the furniture. They were meant to protect the furniture, except they were so old, they were stained and dusty themselves.

Zack stood before a portrait in a gilded frame. It was faded with age, but he could still tell that the woman in the painting was beautiful. "Is that her?" he wondered out loud. "Is that the ghost of Suite 613?"

Across the room, London stood transfixed in front of a broken mirror. Usually, when London looked in a mirror, she was staring lovingly at her own reflection. Now, she was wondering if maybe it was *the* broken mirror.

Maddie had opened the drapes on the window and was inspecting the gargoyles outside. Gargoyles were supposedly meant to ward off evil. Maddie wasn't superstitious, but she wondered whether these gargoyles had done their job.

"Do you hear a noise?" asked London, looking away from the mirror for a moment. She was talking about a click-clicking sound. *Click, click, click*. It sounded like chattering.

"It's Cody's teeth!" Zack crowed, as they all turned toward the entryway where Cody was still hovering.

Zack went over to his brother, and not-so-gently clamped his hand under Cody's chin to stop the noise. Maddie was kinder. "Cody, trust me, there is no ghost here causing weird things to happen," she reassured him.

Just then, Maddie spied something on the ground.

"There is no ghost, but I do see a purse!" she yelped, then reached over to snag London's lost purse. "Finders keepers! Losers weepers!" she roared in triumph.

In less than a second, London was standing threateningly over Maddie. "Hand me the loot, or you get the boot," she seethed. Begrudgingly, Maddie handed it over. London reclaimed her purse, pleased to discover the leather still felt buttery soft and expensive to the touch. Yet when she opened it, she discovered . . . there was nothing there.

"The ghost stole my money," she whined, stamping her foot. She looked around the room for the object of her anger. "She is so dead!"

Heavy footsteps echoed throughout the room. *Thud. Thud. Thud.*

"It's the ghost." London's voice had started to quiver.

Thud. Thud. Thud.

It wasn't often that London apologized. But it seemed that Irene, the ghost of Suite 613, got special treatment. "Sorry about the whole dead thing!" London called out.

Thud. Thud. Thud.

Apparently, Irene didn't accept London's apology.

The group stood in stony silence. Where were the noises coming from? What was going to happen next?

Cody couldn't take the suspense. "London, save me!" he cried, hurling himself at the person closest to him. Unfortunately, it was also the person least likely to catch him. London neglected to hold her arms out, and poor Cody went crashing to the floor, landing smack on his butt.

Thud. Thud. Thud.

The thuds were coming closer. And closer. So close, they were coming from . . . the door to Suite 613!

The group let out a collective scream: *"AHHHHHHHHHH!"* And then, the door opened, and in walked the hotel manager, Mr. Moseby. He was holding his ears as he entered the suite.

"Thank you," he said sarcastically. "I

will bill you for the hearing aid I now require. I could hear you screaming from the lobby."

"Mr. Moseby," Zack's voice had an unfamiliar crack, "have *you* ever seen the ghost?"

"There is no ghost," replied Mr. Moseby swiftly, his eyes darting across the room.

Maddie cast a told-you-so look at the rest of the group. Why were they all such scaredy-cats?

Except clearly Mr. Moseby *did* think there was a ghost, because the next thing he said was: "Now, let's leave before *she* gets annoyed."

By *she* Mr. Moseby meant Irene. A slip of the tongue had given him away.

So there *is* a ghost in Suite 613, thought Zack. It was then that he had another one of his brilliant ideas. It wasn't a prank this time. It was blackmail. His third target of the day? Mr. Moseby.

He faced the hotel manager and said in his most fearless tone: "Tell us about the ghost. Or we might have to ask you again in the lobby . . . when people are checking in."

Mr. Moseby fidgeted for a few moments; Zack guessed he was weighing his options. Finally, he realized he didn't have any options. "Very well," he said with a defeated sigh. And so the group gathered around Mr. Moseby to hear the story of Irene, the ghost in Suite 613.

Chapter 5

Mr. Moseby may not have wanted to tell the story, but once he started, he couldn't help getting into it. He knew he had his audience's rapt attention, and he milked it for all it was worth. "It was a long time ago. I had just started working at the Tipton as a bellhop. It was a dark and stormy night, and I was working diligently."

It was hard to imagine Mr. Moseby as a

bellhop, let alone *young*. But Zack, Cody, London, and Maddie did their best to visualize his story in their heads. Here's how it went:

Mr. Moseby was working late and feeling tired, so he decided to take a nap in a vacant room. The room he picked? Suite 613. "I had heard rumors about 613," Mr. Moseby recollected, "but I didn't believe in ghosts." He entered the room and was shocked by what he discovered. "I felt a sudden rush of cold air, followed by an overpowering aroma of pizza."

Pizza? thought his puzzled listeners.

Young Mr. Moseby realized he was not only tired, he was also hungry. "Mmmmmm, pizza," young Mr. Moseby said to himself. "I could dig a slice."

Except young Mr. Moseby was not alone in the room. Because someone, a woman who he couldn't see, responded to him! "I hate pizza," boomed the woman's cranky, craggy voice. "It reminds me of my unfaithful husband."

Young Mr. Moseby thought he might be hearing things! He was very tired, after all. Maybe he was smelling things, too. He *was* very hungry. Or maybe he was just going crazy. A strange angry woman's voice? The delicious scent of pizza? What was going on?

And then, something even stranger happened. A silver hairbrush went flying through the room, crashing into the already broken mirror. Young Mr. Moseby ducked to avoid being smacked in the head by a brush. He'd asked for a slice. He didn't want to *be* sliced!

A wind swept through the suite, and young Mr. Moseby, now wide awake and frightened for his life, went tearing out of the suite and into the hallway. He never looked back.

Mr. Moseby shook his head, remembering that perilous night. "I did injure my ankle," he added softly, wincing at the painful memory. "I was never able to boogie-oogie again."

They sat in silent contemplation, stunned by the story Mr. Moseby had just told, and reeling from the news that he'd never "boogie-oogie again." (Or maybe it was just imagining him boogie-oogie-ing in the first place that left them all speechless.) No one said a word for several seconds, which made it all the more shocking when a ghostly apparition jumped out at them!

"*Booooooo!*" yelled the ghost.

"*Aghhhhhhh!!*" yelled the group.

Apparently the ghost could smell fear, because it went directly for Cody, and lunged. Scrambling to get away, Cody prayed for his life, and frantically clawed his attacker. He slapped and swiped until suddenly the ghostly apparition revealed itself to be Zack. With a white dust cloth over his head.

"That was awesome! You should have seen your faces!" Zack guffawed, throwing the dust cloth off him. A cloud of dust billowed in the air. Zack turned to his brother and smirked. "Oh, wait, I can show you *your* face," he teased, contorting his face to look exactly like Cody's terrified one. He even mocked the way Cody had fought him, slapping the air frantically.

"Let's see what my hand looks like when it squishes your face!" Cody hollered. Then he chased his brother out of Suite 613.

Chapter 6

"I wasn't scared," growled Cody as they entered the suite—their *own* suite—several minutes later.

"If you weren't scared, why were you shaking in the elevator?" countered Zack.

"Because it hasn't been inspected in three years! Don't you read that little card?"

I really *am* the fearless brother, thought Zack. "Well, I want to see the ghost," he told Cody. "So, I dare you to spend the night with me in Suite 613. Five bucks says you run out first."

Five bucks wasn't much when you compared it to London's weekly allowance, but it was a lot to Zack and Cody.

Scared as he was, Cody was not about to let his brother spook him so easily. "I'd take that bet," he said, responding to his brother's challenge, "but Mom'll never let us do it."

Zack and Cody's mom had a knack for making timely entrances. "Darn right I won't," she said as she walked into the room. "Do what?"

"Camp out tonight in Suite 613," Zack told her.

"Otherwise known as the haunted room," Cody added.

Carey didn't exactly like the sound of

that. Then again, what mother would? "Well—" she stammered.

Cody couldn't help feeling relieved. "So that's a no," he said. "We accept your wise and carefully considered decision."

Oh, please! thought Zack. "You just don't want to go because you're chicken."

"She said no," said Cody, unusually pleased to back up his mother's orders. "And no means no, mister. Don't make her say it again!"

"*Cluck, cluck, cluck!*" clucked Zack, doing a chicken dance around the room.

"Zack, no brother-clucking!" Carey said sternly.

"So can we go?" asked Zack, who was convinced he could turn his mother around.

"I don't think so," Carey replied.

Then, Zack had another idea. Why, his ideas were getting craftier by the minute!

"What if we got Maddie and London to stay with us?" he asked. After all, Maddie and London were really old. Fifteen years old! Maddie babysat for them pretty often.

Carey thought about it for a second. "Well, I guess that would be okay," she said.

Cody couldn't believe his ears! His brother was a master manipulator! And what was up with his mother? How could she be so easily fooled? "You know, you don't have to give in to him," Cody balked. "What kind of mother are you?"

Apparently, Carey was taking this opportunity to teach her son something. Plus, she had to get to rehearsal and needed this conversation to end. "Cody, you do whatever you want, but there's no such thing as ghosts. If there were, my mother-in-law would still be haunting me."

With that, she was gone.

"So, you gonna spend the night finger-painting with Mommy?" baby-talked Zack.

Cody stared at his brother. He was not giving up without a fight. He puffed his chest out and, with uncharacteristic courage, declared: "No, I'm gonna spend the night in Suite 613. Then when you run out first, I'm gonna spend your five bucks."

"We'll see about that," said Zack with a laugh.

We *will* see about that, thought Cody as he tried to erase all the terrified thoughts from his brain.

The brothers shook on it.

Chapter 7

The night hadn't yet begun, but Zack was already planning how he'd spend Cody's five bucks. Well, actually he hadn't come up with a plan yet. He was torn between spending it on comic books or candy. Then again, maybe he'd save it toward a bigger purchase like a cell phone or a video game.

Maddie and the twins trudged down the gloomy hallway toward Suite 613, and Zack couldn't believe how lucky he'd gotten. It was storming outside. Storms always made things scarier. He glanced at Cody, all wide-eyed, his "blankie" in hand. This was going to be the easiest five bucks Zack ever scored!

"London said she'd meet us here with the passkey," said Maddie once they'd gotten to the door. "She just had to pick up a few things."

Apparently, to London, a few things meant anything that might fit into a gigantic steamer trunk—and Esteban.

"Sorry, I'm late. It's Esteban's fault," said London when she finally breezed down the hallway.

"Yes," wheezed Esteban, as he strained under the weight of the giant luggage. "My hernia . . . my fault." Apparently, even though Esteban was suffering, he could still be sarcastic.

"I thought you said you were going to rough it," Maddie said, shaking her head. Sometimes she couldn't believe she was friends with London. Sometimes she couldn't believe she *knew* London.

"I only brought my overnight bag," London defended herself.

"Please forgive me for delaying our spooky yet fun adventure with ghosties," Esteban said.

"There is no ghost," Maddie corrected him. What was wrong with these people?

"Is so!" contended London. "And I'm willing to rough it all night to prove it to you. Here's the key."

"Here goes nothing," groaned Maddie.

"Here goes my lower back," moaned Esteban.

They entered Suite 613 for the second time that day.

❖❖❖

"This isn't so scary," said Cody brightly when they entered the room. But then a sudden bolt of lightning and a clap of thunder said otherwise. The room went black, and the group fumbled around to see where they were. "Okay, now it is," Cody gasped.

And it was about to get scarier! They were still trying to get their bearings when the door to the hall burst open, and a blinding blast of fluorescent light filled the entryway. In the center of the light was the silhouette of a man holding what appeared to be an extremely large club.

An extremely large club!

"It's the ghost!" yelled Cody.

"And it's holding a club!" yelled London.

"And now it's eating the club!" yelled back Cody.

They blinked into the weird glow to get a closer look. Ohhhhh! The ghost *wasn't* eating his club. In fact, he wasn't even a ghost. He was Arwin, the hotel handyman, holding a flashlight under his face while eating a foot-long sandwich. "It's not a club, it's a sub," mumbled Arwin through a mouthful of sandwich. "Meatball marinara. Want some?"

For some reason, London was still screaming in terror.

"What's so scary about a sandwich?" Maddie asked her.

"The guy who's eating it," replied London with a shudder. And then, because she had a tendency to be very blunt, London turned to Arwin and said, "I just think you're kinda creepy. No offense."

Apparently Arwin was used to this. "None taken," he said with a shrug. "Lot of women say that. Including Mother."

Arwin fixed the circuit breaker, and soon the lights came back on. "See, the ghost didn't knock out the lights," Maddie assured her friends. "The storm did. Right, Arwin?"

"No, it was the ghost," replied Arwin. He wasn't a man who minced words.

Arwin lugged a large, oddly scientific-looking contraption into the room. It was a cross between a robot and a vacuum cleaner, and apparently it would help him see the ghost. "I've been trying to see the ghost for years," Arwin explained. "But tonight, tonight is my golden opportunity."

"Why?" asked Cody, who couldn't help showing off how well he was doing in science this year. "Because the lightning provides sufficient atmospheric ozone, allowing your instrument to pick up any ectoplasmic manifestations?"

Arwin didn't pause to decipher what Cody had just said. Instead, he answered simply: "No, because Mother's at bingo and I don't have to be home until ten." He dragged his machine around the room, trying to pick up a reading.

"Whooaa, Nellie!" he screamed as the machine began beeping and sputtering; now it was pulling *him* across the room. "Okay, we got about twenty scary abnormalities in this room! Granted, nineteen of 'em are me, but still—"

Arwin approached the portrait of the ghost of Suite 613, and his machine started to smoke. Then it turned red. And then, the woman in the picture—Irene, the ghost of Suite 613—moved. She moved!

"Did you see that?" stammered Cody.

"You mean the face moving and the eyes looking?" gasped London, who clearly wished she hadn't seen what she'd seen. "No."

"Me neither," shuddered Cody.

"I did!" clamored Arwin, sounding petrified. "And there's a scary ghost in here, and she's mad!" Arwin made a mad dash for the door. They could hear him screaming "Mommy!!!" from down the hall.

The next shriek of panic came from London, who would have followed Arwin out the door, except she didn't want to leave without her "weekend bag." Too bad it was a steamer trunk. London tried to haul it toward the door, only it was massive, she was teensy in comparison, and it wouldn't budge. "Help?" she asked, sending Esteban a pleading look.

But something had dawned on Esteban. "Yes, that's what we must do," he said leaping up. "We must help."

London thought he meant they'd all help with the steamer trunk. "Thanks," she chirped. "You guys take each side. I'll supervise."

But that was *not* what Esteban had in mind. "I meant we must help the poor tormented ghostie cross over to a better place."

"You mean like the St. Mark's Hotel? Where they pay overtime?" asked Maddie, who even in trying times was still thinking about her meager wages.

"This is not a joking matter," said Esteban solemnly.

"Obviously, you haven't seen my paycheck," quipped Maddie.

But Esteban was serious, *deadly* serious. "I know how to contact the spirit world," he said.

Zack couldn't believe it. "You do?"

"Of course," said Esteban, who was no

longer wasting time. "Shall we begin?"

"It's okay, Blankie," Cody murmured to the fraying old blanket he was clutching. "We'll get through this together."

But would they?

Chapter 8

Esteban rescued a leopard-print scarf from London's trunk, then wrapped it around his head turban style. He gathered the group around the table. "Is everyone ready to call the spirit?" he asked. Esteban reached for the candle on the table. He was going to light it. But, before he could, it burst into flame. The candle had lit itself! The group stared, stunned. "Apparently the spirit is calling us," Esteban remarked.

"Hey, guys! Watch this," Zack said as he pointed the remote control in the direction of Esteban.

"Man, that was awesome!" hooted Zack, after he'd embarrassed Esteban.

"Don't tell me," London groaned,
"you saw the ghost in Suite 613."

"It's the ghost," gasped London, ducking
behind Cody for protection.

The group let out a collective scream:
"AHHHHHHHHHH!"

"I want to see the ghost," Zack told Cody. "So, I
dare you to spend the night with me in Suite 613.
Five bucks says you run out first."

"I'd take that bet," Cody said, responding to his brother's challenge, "but Mom'll never let us do it."

"Silence, please," Esteban commanded. Everyone joined hands. "Ghostie, if I may call you that, speak to us."

"Tell her we're not home," said Cody.

Esteban ignored this. "Silence, please," he commanded. Everyone joined hands. "Be very still, but relaxed," Esteban instructed. "Ghostie, if I may call you that, speak to us."

Maddie didn't wait for the ghost to speak. Instead, she interrupted to call them all gullible dopes.

Esteban reacted very dramatically to this. And strangely, too. "Disbelievers will be punished!" he declared in a voice that didn't sound like his own.

"Ooh, I'm *soooo* scared," mocked Maddie.

Maddie's chair started to shake, then suddenly zoomed back a few feet—with her in it! The invisible force moving the chair wasn't being too gentle.

"Ooh, I'm so scared," whispered Maddie. Only this time she sounded like she meant it.

Now, even fearless Zack was thrown. "You are?" he asked Maddie in a halting voice.

"Spirit . . . hear me!" cried Esteban. "I am calling you!"

There was silence. Then, a loud humming noise filled the room. It took the group several seconds to realize the humming noise was, in fact, coming from Esteban! "What's going on?!" London asked him. Esteban explained he was on hold.

First, Esteban started to shake; then the whole table started to shake. Thunder filled the suite, and lightning ricocheted from wall to wall. The candle on the table went out. And then, the table itself began to rise.

"Either the table is getting higher, or the floor is getting lower," remarked Cody.

"She's heeeeeeeeeeeere! *Hola*, ghostie!" shrieked Esteban. "Welcome to our—"

And then something happened to Esteban.

He began to twitch as if he had no control over his own body. He smacked his head on the table. *Boom!* And then, when he arose, he was no longer Esteban.

He was Irene, the ghost of Suite 613!

"Who dares to call me in the afterlife?" shrieked Irene.

No one knew what to say. Cody turned to Zack. If he was *so* bold, *so* fearless, he should take this one. "It's for you," he told his brother.

"Are you the ghost of Irene?" asked Zack in a voice barely above a whisper.

"Yes." Esteban's lips quivered as the ghost spoke through him. "My spirit is doomed to languish in agony for all eternity."

London had put her fears to rest in favor of more important matters. "Whatever," she told Irene. "Listen, ummm, could I get my thousand dollars back?"

"You will be silent!" shrieked Irene.

This woman was rude, a fact that irritated Maddie. "What is your problem, lady?!" she wanted to know.

"I was betrayed, so I am angry," said the ghost. If she was going to say more, they'd never know. Because suddenly, a silver hairbrush was flying through the air toward the mirror. It crashed, sending shards of mirror into the air.

Everyone ducked for cover. They hovered underneath the table for several seconds, then emerged, shaken, to discover the room had been overtaken by an unmistakable odor. What was it? London sniffed the air, scrunched up her nostrils, and asked what everyone else was thinking: "Does anyone smell . . . pizza?"

"Don't ever say that word!" commanded the ghost in a booming voice. Boy, she was really doing a number on poor Esteban's vocal cords.

Maddie felt like she'd had enough. "I love pizza!" she told the ghost. "What are you gonna do about it?"

Apparently, the ghost was up for a challenge. Seconds later, Esteban was clapping his hands. A peal of thunder roared outside. And Maddie's chair went careening into the darkness.

She had disappeared.

"Maddie, no!" screamed Zack.

"Wh-wh-wh-wh-where did she go?" London stammered.

Clearly, the ghost wanted them to know she wasn't kidding around. "Anyone else have anything to say?" the possessed Esteban demanded.

"N-n-n-n-not me," stuttered Cody. "I hate pizza."

Oh, no!

Why had he said the word?

Cody clapped his hand over his mouth, realizing his mistake, but it was too late. His blankie was ripped from his clutches and sent flying into the air. "Blankie!! Nooooo!!!" shrieked Cody, bounding out of his chair and after his beloved blankie. *"Ahhhhhhhhh!"* he screamed.

Soon, he, too, had disappeared into the darkness.

This was more than even Zack could take. "Cody? Buddy? Oh, man! Mom's not gonna like this!"

London had, once again, returned her attention to more important matters at hand. "Listen, Irene, I hate to be a nudge, but about that thousand dollars—"

Talk about asking for it! As suddenly as Maddie and Cody had disappeared, so did

London, sucked backward into the darkness. "I'll take a check!!!" were her last words.

Now it was only Zack and Esteban at the table. "Esteban!" Zack sounded desperate. "Hang up on her! Hang up," he begged.

But it was too late for that. Esteban had a funny look on his face and a menacing stare. "Esteban's gone," he said ominously. "Say *adios*, *amigo*. Ayayayaayay!"

Lightning flashed, thunder bellowed, and before he knew it, Zack was all alone. The window drapes billowed as a cold wind rushed through the room. Zack had to get out! Terrified, he scurried toward the door. Only the knob, it wouldn't turn! He shook it frantically, until . . .

. . . the knob came off in his hand!

How would he get out now???

The window! Zack ran to open it. But what he saw outside Suite 613 was even scarier than what was inside. The gargoyles had swiveled to face him, their eyes fired up like jack-o'-lanterns.

Zack staggered back into the room, the gargoyles' eyes following him. "They're coming to get you," screeched Irene. Only now she was no longer inhabiting Esteban, she was in . . . the portrait!!

The portrait!?! The portrait was talking? Without believing it, without thinking what he was doing, Zack reached his hand out to touch the picture of the woman's face. Only it reached out before he could, and grabbed him—by the nose. "Got your nose!" the ghost screeched.

Before Zack could get his bearings, before he could even check to see if he still had his nose, another undead creature entered the room. It was a glowing floating skeleton. "Did you order room service?" bellowed the skeleton. "I brought you ribs. Ha-ha-ha!"

Apparently the skeleton thought his joke was really funny. Because he laughed so hard, his head fell off.

"Hey, what's the matter? You don't have to lose your head! Hahahaha!"

A gust of wind swooped through the room, blowing the front door open. Knowing this might be his last opportunity to get out alive, Zack made a break for the door before it was too late.

Chapter 9

Zack had been expecting to leave with Cody's five bucks. He hadn't been expecting to leave without Cody! A million thoughts raced through his head as he exited Suite 613. Like, how was he going to break it to Mom? What would life be like without Cody? Or Maddie? Or London? Or Esteban?

But Zack had more pressing concerns at the moment. Because before he could make a run for it, a giant spider dropped down from the ceiling. It was massive and hairy and really, really gross! It was probably poisonous, too. Zack wasn't as good in science as Cody, but he remembered that there were different types of poisonous spiders, like scorpions and tarantulas. Zack screamed. But no one was there to hear him. With nowhere else to run, a petrified Zack returned to Suite 613.

But Suite 613 had new guests. Ghosts. Four ghosts. And they were heading straight for Zack.

"*Boo!!!*" shouted the ghosts.

"*Ahhhhhhhhhhhh!*" shrieked Zack.

Little did Zack know he was in for the biggest shock of his life! Because, suddenly, the ghosts were throwing off their sheets to reveal they weren't ghosts. They were Cody, Esteban, Maddie, and London, and this had all been an elaborate—a *very* elaborate—practical joke.

"Gotcha!" hooted Cody. "That'll be five bucks."

"But . . ." Zack was still reeling from everything that had happened to him. He felt very confused.

"Special effects, courtesy of Arwin Q. Hochhauser," announced Cody as he motioned toward the closet. Arwin emerged carrying the skeleton. He took a bow.

Arwin demonstrated how he'd made all the spooky things happen. He pressed a button on his remote to show Zack how he made the table levitate. Another button made the windows rattle. A third made the front door open and close.

Meanwhile, Maddie pulled a large pizza from underneath the sofa. "Anyone for pizza?" she asked with a grin.

Zack couldn't believe this! He'd been had. Totally had! "You guys are mean!" he whined.

"We're sorry, Zack," Maddie said. "But you've played so many practical jokes on us, we just want to show you how it feels."

"Yes," added Esteban. "Forgive me, my little friend, but you should not have made me the butt of the gassy-noises joke. Most of which were not mine."

Arwin reminded Zack about the time he'd put itching powder in his coveralls. London complained about the time Zack had sent her a fake love letter from the movie star Orlando Bloom. Except then Maddie admitted that she'd pulled that prank.

"Well, the joke was all on you guys," boasted Zack. He'd regained some of his composure. "Because I wasn't really scared."

But Cody wasn't going to let him get away with a lie. "Yeah, right!" he balked, rolling his eyes. "You should have seen your face. Oh, wait, I can show you your face!" This time Cody contorted his face to look exactly like Zack's terrified one.

Zack had taken all the humiliation he could take. Cody was going to pay for this! He chased his brother out of the room.

Chapter 10

Who should Zack and Cody run into in the hallway but their mother and Mr. Moseby.

"Mr. Moseby," Carey was saying, "I was in the middle of a third encore. Why do you need me?"

"Mom! Stop him!" shrieked Cody.

Zack chased Cody in a circle around Carey.

"Zack . . . Zack . . . Zack! Stop right

now!" Cary demanded. "What did you do to your brother?"

"Nothing! He scared me!" tattled Zack.

Carey couldn't help feeling pleasantly surprised to hear this news. "He did?" Realizing how this sounded, she turned to Cody, then tried to act extra stern. "I mean, you did?"

A woman emerged from a hotel room. She looked more than a little irked. Apparently, *she'd* called Mr. Moseby to complain about the noise. And knowing that, as always, the source of the noise was Zack and Cody, Mr. Moseby had called Carey. "Thank you for coming up, Mr. Moseby," said the guest.

"I assume this is the ruckus to which you were referring?" said Mr. Moseby, pointing his finger at Cody and Zack.

Zack and Cody still had their own battle

to settle, and they ignored Mr. Moseby's accusation. "Cody played a really mean practical joke on me, Mommy!" Zack complained, snuggling up to his mother for a comforting hug.

Over his head, Carey couldn't help smiling appreciatively at Cody. She was proud of him for being fearless. Still, she knew she had to reprimand him. "Cody, shame on you! Tell your brother you're sorry. Shame on you."

"Sorry, Zack," muttered Cody not-too-convincingly. He couldn't miss an opportunity to rub it in some more. "You're such a chicken!" he told his brother. "I can't believe you got scared over a little ghost!"

"This hotel has a ghost?" asked the guest, who'd clearly forgotten what she'd called the hotel manager to complain about.

"Of course not," spat Mr. Moseby, glaring

at Zack and Cody. "Now, tell the nice lady you were just pretending."

"Yeah, there's no ghost," said Cody.

"Oh, that's too bad," replied the guest thoughtfully, "because a lot of people would pay extra to stay in a haunted room."

"Ohhhhh, he meant, no ghost out in the *hallway*," said Mr. Moseby, who'd do or say anything to please a guest. "However, the *room* is lousy with ghosts. The rest of the hotel is haunted by these two."

He meant Zack and Cody, of course.

Chapter 11

Zack couldn't believe he was doing this again. After that night, he'd sworn up and down he'd never return to Suite 613.

But here he was entering the suite, which was still as gloomy as ever. Zack hoped he wasn't being suckered. "Did you really leave your blankie here?" he asked Cody. "Or is this just another stupid prank?"

"Listen, I don't kid when it comes to Blankie," answered Cody. "Now help me look around. Unless you're too scared."

Scared? Please! thought Zack.

They began to scavenge the room when, all of a sudden, they realized they weren't alone. There was a beautiful woman in the suite, too! A woman who looked familiar, yet they were sure they'd never seen her before. She was wearing an old-fashioned dress; her skin was porcelain white; her lips the color of the brightest red crayon. "Excuse me," said the woman, tapping Cody on the shoulder. "Is this yours?" She was holding Cody's blankie.

"Yeah, thanks," murmured Cody, a little shocked, taking his blanket.

"Don't mention it," said the woman. She then turned toward the wall, stepped into the portrait, and disappeared.

Cody and Zack took one look at each other and screamed. There wouldn't be another visit to Suite 613 for a very long time! Maybe Zack was usually the tougher brother, the one who readily took dares and who didn't think twice before challenging Cody to spend the night in Suite 613. But when it came to seeing a real-live ghost face-to-face, he was just as scared as Cody.

Don't miss the next story about Zack and Cody

Zack Attack

Adapted by M.C. King

Based on the television series, "The Suite Life of Zack & Cody", created by Danny Kallis & Jim Geogha

Based on the episode written by Bill Freiberger

Every home has its own set of rules. Zack and Cody Martin's home was no exception. Only their home was the Tipton, the most luxurious hotel in Boston.

Zack and Cody knew they weren't supposed to play basketball in the Tipton's lobby, which was grand, to say the least. But there was something so satisfying about dribbling the ball on the hard marble floors. And when Zack tossed the ball to Cody, the antique chandeliers made a really cool clinking sound.

Zack and Cody lived at the Tipton because their mother, Carey, was the lounge singer there. If Carey wasn't working, she was often rehearsing, leaving the rule-enforcing to the other people who worked in the hotel. The Tipton's manager, Mr. Moseby, was the biggest stickler for rules.

Mr. Moseby had a habit of seeing and hearing everything. And within seconds of Zack and Cody entering the hotel, he appeared before them—just as Cody was throwing the ball to Zack. Despite his constricting fancy uniform, Mr. Moseby was quick: he caught the basketball in midair. He held on to it, shaking his head disagreeably at the two boys. "No b-ball today," he said with a grimace. "Game has been canceled on the account of . . . this is a hotel."

Cody shuffled his feet shamefully during the scolding. He and Zack were twins, but he was the younger of the two and also the more rule-abiding. He didn't relish getting in trouble, like Zack did.

The Tipton was not only fancy, it was also one of the largest hotels in Boston. Businesses often rented conference rooms for meetings or held special events in the ballrooms. Usually, the events were *really* boring. Take last week's annual podiatrist convention. Cody had needed to look "podiatrist" up in the dictionary to discover what it meant: a doctor who specialized in feet. (Who'd wanna specialize in feet?)

So Zack and Cody were very surprised

when Mr. Moseby cut short his lecture on no basketball in the lobby to say: "Now listen up. *Go Dance USA* is coming to the Tipton for their local broadcast. And it is my greatest wish that you do not scare them away with your antics or . . ." He wriggled his nose in dissatisfaction at Zack and Cody's sweaty after-school clothes. ". . . your odor."

Zack and Cody couldn't believe it. *Go Dance USA* was one of the best shows on television! "We'll do our best not to stink, Mr. Moseby," promised Zack.

"Splendid," Mr. Moseby replied wearily, and walked away.

Zack and Cody's friend Max had come home with them after school. It just so happened that Max was the best dancer at their school, so she was even more excited than the twins to hear Mr. Moseby's announcement. "I can't believe *Go Dance USA* is coming here. I've wanted to go on that show since I was a kid!" Max went to check out the *Go Dance USA* poster that had been put up in honor of the event; the twins followed.

"Max, you have to enter that contest," said Cody. "You're better than that girl in the Missy Elliot video."

"I know, this could be my big break!" Max said dreamily. She took a moment to examine the poster. The rules for participants were listed at the bottom. Oops, they'd missed one detail. "But it's for couples," Max informed the boys. "Zack, would you be my partner?"

Cody couldn't believe his ears! Here he'd been talking Max up, and she was choosing Zack as her partner! Without even considering Cody? "Him?" Cody balked incredulously, motioning to Zack. "What about the guy who just said how good you are?"

"Do you dance?" Max asked Cody.

Did he dance?!? "I love to dance!" exclaimed Cody.

"Too bad you're no good," teased Zack. "I'll be your partner," he offered Max. "I'd love to be on TV. And I've got the face for it."

Oh, please! thought Cody. "I have the same face!" he argued.

"Yeah, but your face can't dance," said Zack.

Arrrgh! Zack could be so full of himself sometimes! Who did he think he was? Why, Cody oughta . . . An angry Cody took a step toward his brother.

Max took it upon herself to break the brothers up. "Boys, please," she begged. "We'll have a fair and impartial audition. Zack, let's see what you got."

Zack was happy for the chance. "Check it," he told Cody, and launched into a series of music-video–style hip-hop moves.

"Yeah?" said Cody, certain he could top that. "Well, watch this." Cody did a version of the robot—if the robot was a total spaz. He ended up lying face forward on the lobby carpet. Cody might be a fighter, but he knew when to give up. "Good luck in the dance contest, guys," he mumbled.

The SuiteLife of Zack & Cody

Check out these other books based on *The Suite Life of Zack & Cody!*

Double Trouble

PHOTOS FROM THE SHOW INSIDE!

From the hit TV series on Disney C

Do Not Disturb

Hotel and Resorts

4 pages of full-color photos inside!

Room of Doom

PHOTOS FROM THE SHOW INSIDE!

From the hit TV series on Disney Channel

Available wherever books are sold!

DISNEY PRESS